FATAL VERSE
COLE STEELE

ONE

Lori Tolliver stood in her small, cramped office, staring out the window at the bustling Nashville street below. The melody of a nearby street performer's guitar drifted in through the open window, mixing with the hum of passing cars and the chatter of pedestrians. As the city pulsed with life, she couldn't help but feel a sense of pride in the law practice she had built from the ground up. It was here, in the heart of Music City, that Lori and her brother Shaun were determined to fight for justice, one case at a time. Little did she know that her next client would challenge everything she believed in.

The door to Lori's office creaked open, drawing her attention away from the window. Shaun entered, his piercing blue eyes scanning the room as he tossed a manila envelope onto her cluttered desk. "Got something that might interest you, sis," he said, his voice a mix of curiosity and caution. Lori raised an eyebrow, intrigued by the seriousness in her brother's tone. Picking up the envelope, she carefully opened it and pulled out the contents: a collection of newspaper clippings detailing the high-profile murder case of wealthy businessman John Parker. As she skimmed through the headlines, a knot formed in the pit of her stomach. She knew taking on a case like this would thrust her and Shaun into the public eye, testing their skills and resolve like never before. But she also knew that if there was even a shred of doubt about John Parker's guilt, it was their duty to uncover the truth and fight for justice, no matter the cost.

Shaun leaned against the bookshelf, studying Lori's expression as she read through the newspaper clippings. He knew that despite the risks, this case had the potential to change their lives and solidify their place among Nashville's top legal professionals. "So, what do you think?" he asked, crossing his arms over his chest. Lori set the clippings down and looked up at her brother, her gaze filled with determination. "This case won't be easy, Shaun. There's a lot at stake, not just for us, but for

John Parker and the victim's family as well," she said, her voice firm and unwavering. She took a deep breath, steeling herself for the challenges that lay ahead. "But if there's a chance that we can expose the truth and bring justice to those who deserve it, then we have to try." Together, they shared a solemn nod, knowing that this case would test their professional limits. They would quickly discover that in the world of Nashville's legal scene, nothing was ever as it seemed.

TWO

John Parker was the CEO of Omni Associates, a company nestled in a high-rise building in downtown Nashville. The company, founded by his great-grandfather, had a long history of securing military contracts from the federal government, supplying logistical support to troops during the Vietnam War and beyond. Global conflict had always been good for business and the Parker family.

His office was located in the AT&T Building, also known as the "Batman Building" due to its distinctive architecture resembling the superhero's mask. Towering over the city at 617 feet, the 33-story building offered a stunning view of the Nashville skyline and the Cumberland River.

Upon exiting the rocket-like elevator that had carried her dozens of floors above the beautifully landscaped grounds, Lori Tolliver was immediately greeted by John's executive assistant, Kate Shields. Kate directed her to a conference room and asked, "Would you care for something to drink? We have virtually everything available." Lori responded with a smile, "Coffee would be nice. Thank you."

The conference room exuded opulence, from the plush leather chairs to the immaculate temperature and humidity control that ensured absolute comfort. Lori removed her legal pad from her satchel and set it down on the polished mahogany table.

John Parker knocked before entering the room. He possessed a square jawline and was in his early forties, with no signs of gray in his medium brown hair. His brown eyes held a penetrating gaze that seemed to take in everything. His slim build belied a sense of strength, as if he could handle himself in a fight. There wasn't an ounce of fat on his frame.

"Good morning, are we ready?" John asked as he entered the room. Lori nodded. "I thought we'd get an early start." John replied, "This worked out well, I didn't have much on my schedule today." He took a seat across from Lori just as Kate returned with a cup of coffee on a saucer and a small basket containing creamers and sweeteners.

Parker's assistant closed the door behind her as she left, leaving Lori and John alone to discuss the impending case that would test their mettle and force them to confront the murky underbelly of Nashville's elite.

THREE

Lori held her pen at the ready. "Tell me again where you were on the day she was found and the day prior," she inquired, her gaze steady and unyielding.

John Parker thought for a moment, rubbing his chin. "The day before is the easy part. I was here at the office until about six, then went home for dinner."

"And what about when she was found?" Lori prodded.

"We were at this hole-in-the-wall club where she got her start," John replied.

"You were with her?" Lori asked, her eyebrows rising in surprise.

"Yes, at the Blue Bird," John confirmed. "Didn't she sign a recording contract?"

"Yeah, we liked to hang out there. Hiding in plain sight. No one knew she had a deal anywhere," John explained, a hint of nostalgia in his voice.

"Obviously, you weren't worried about getting found out," Lori observed.

John shrugged. "My wife and I have a sort of arrangement. She likes the country club and golf."

"You like entertainment, I got it," Lori said, trying to keep the conversation focused. "Do you find it strange?"

"What goes on in a relationship behind closed doors isn't any of my business," Lori stated matter-of-factly, "except when your client is being charged for murder."

"So, your wife wouldn't be jealous?" Lori inquired.

"Of course, she would," John admitted, "spices it up a little. But not to the point where she'd contemplate killing someone because of it. Myself included."

As Lori scribbled down John's account of his whereabouts, she couldn't help but feel the weight of the case bearing down on her. With each new detail that emerged, the task of proving John's innocence seemed increasingly daunting.

FOUR

Lori and Shaun visited the Blue Bird, the club where John claimed to have been with the victim on the night she was murdered. The club's dim lighting and intimate atmosphere offered a stark contrast to the glitz and glamour of Nashville's mainstream music scene.

While questioning the club's staff and regulars, they discovered that John's presence at the Blue Bird on the night in question went largely unnoticed. It was as if he and Ashley Brenner had truly been hiding in plain sight, just as he had described. This neither confirmed nor disproved John's alibi, but it gave Lori and Shaun a starting point for their investigation.

Meanwhile, the prosecution was building a seemingly airtight case against John. They had witnesses who claimed to have seen him arguing with the victim on multiple occasions, and financial records that suggested he may have had a motive to silence her. As the evidence against John mounted, Lori knew they had to dig deeper to find any inconsistencies that could help exonerate him.

In their search for the truth, Lori and Shaun began to uncover a web of secrets and lies that extended far beyond John Parker and his relationship with the victim. They discovered that the victim, an up-and-coming singer-songwriter, had connections to several prominent figures in the Nashville music industry, some of whom stood to lose a great deal if her career took off.

As they chased down leads and interviewed potential witnesses, Lori and Shaun found themselves navigating a treacherous world of ambition, jealousy, and betrayal. They were constantly reminded that in a city as vibrant and dynamic as Nashville, appearances could be deceiving, and the line between friend and foe was often blurred.

FIVE

Lori and Shaun stood in the victim's apartment, which was decorated with high-end furnishings and elegant décor. The space was neat and orderly, a clear indication that Ashley appreciated the finer things in life. Despite the luxurious surroundings, signs of a violent struggle were evident. A cracked mirror on the wall hinted at the ferocity of the attack, and police tape cordoned off the bedroom where Ashley's life had been brutally taken.

"She put up a fight," said Shaun, examining the scene.

"Her trachea was crushed according to the autopsy," Lori added. "Any defensive wounds?"

"Plenty, but no DNA under her nails or anything. You'd think there'd be some. Anyone grabs you by the throat, I gotta believe you're clawing and scratching to defend yourself."

"Maybe she was caught by surprise and overpowered," Lori suggested. "See if you can talk with her neighbors on the floor."

"I'm sure the detectives already have. You think they're going to talk to me?"

"Use that Tolliver charm of yours. The same one that helped you sell the most mums back in elementary school."

"You remember that?" Shaun smiled.

"I was a little salty watching your class leave for that trip to the zoo."

"That was a great time."

"Really, just going to rub salt in the proverbial wound again?" Lori teased.

"I'm kidding, it wasn't that great. Hardly any of the animals were out that day."

Lori turned to him. "Go talk to the neighbors."

Shaun chuckled. "On it."

He was at the door when she stopped him. "Does this place look like where someone lives while they're trying to make it?"

"A little upscale, if you ask me. Let's dig into this."

Lori walked around the apartment several more times, taking pictures and making mental notes of her observations before leaving. As she closed the door behind her, she couldn't help but feel that there was more to this case than meets the eye. Unraveling the secrets hidden within Ashley's life would be crucial to proving John's innocence and uncovering the truth.

SIX

Shaun Tolliver had knocked on several apartment doors that were on the same floor as Ashley Brenner's. Most of them never answered, and the ones that did had no interest in getting involved. Feeling slightly discouraged, Shaun stood at the elevator, ready to leave when a woman in her forties poked her head out into the hallway, looking both ways.

"Did you just knock?" she asked.

"I did," Shaun replied.

"I was in the shower and thought I heard something. Can I help you with something?"

"Did you know the young lady in 402?" asked Shaun.

"The one that had visitors all hours of the night."

"What do you know about her?"

The woman lowered her voice a bit. "All her male guests were well dressed and much older."

"That's pretty observant," Shaun commented.

"I found it strange, that's all."

"Do you know who she was?"

"No."

"Ever see this guy?" Shaun pulled out his cellphone, scrolled for a few seconds, then showed her a picture of John Parker.

"Yeah, a few times. But there was another one."

"With him?"

"No, alone. Those two would go out late at night, never saw them during the day together."

Shaun's interest was piqued. He thanked the woman for her time and made his way back to Lori. The fact that Ashley had other male visitors, all older and well-dressed, was a significant piece of information. It raised new questions about her relationships and motives.

As Shaun shared the neighbor's observations with Lori, they realized that Ashley's life might have been more complicated than they initially thought. Were these visitors connected to the music industry, or was there another aspect to her life that they had yet to uncover?

SEVEN

Shaun decided to follow up on the information they had gathered from Ashley's apartment and the neighbor's observations. He figured that the management company for the building might have more information on Ashley's background and her relationship with John Parker. With a mix of determination and charm, Shaun managed to convince the woman at the management office to share some details about Ashley's tenancy.

The woman confirmed that Ashley had been a good tenant, always paying her rent on time and causing no disturbances. Shaun pushed further, requesting to see the payment records for Ashley's apartment. The woman hesitated, clearly uncomfortable with sharing that level of detail. Shaun reassured her, explaining the importance of the information to their investigation.

After some more coaxing, the woman relented and pulled up the payment records on her computer. As Shaun looked at the screen, he noticed a familiar name. The records showed that John Parker had been paying Ashley Brenner's rent for the last six months. This new piece of information made it clear that John and Ashley's relationship went beyond casual encounters at the Blue Bird.

Shaun thanked the woman for her help and hurried back to update Lori on his findings. As they discussed the implications of this discovery, they realized that the case was growing more complex. The fact that John had been financially supporting Ashley added another layer to their relationship and could be seen as both a motive for murder and a reason for John to be framed.

Determined to untangle the web of secrets surrounding Ashley's life and death, Lori and Shaun set out to uncover the truth about her relationships, her ambitions, and the people who stood to gain or lose from her success. As they delved deeper into the investigation, they found themselves drawn into a world of intrigue and deception that threatened to shatter the illusion of the glamorous Nashville music scene.

EIGHT

Lori's small office, located in a low-rent district, was a haven of orderliness amidst the chaos outside. Despite the cramped space, everything was meticulously organized and tidy. The worn-out carpet and peeling off-white walls contrasted sharply with Lori's neat arrangement of case files and legal documents. A single window looked out onto the street, but it was perpetually dirty, giving the room a gloomy atmosphere. The landlord had been neglecting necessary repairs, and after months of frustration, Lori had finally threatened legal action.

As a result, a maintenance crew had shown up that day, armed with clipboards and seemingly inspecting the premises. Lori wasn't entirely convinced they would get anything done, but at least it was a start. She and Shaun sat in her office, surrounded by her neatly organized stacks of case files and legal documents, discussing the recent discoveries in Ashley's case.

"So, we have John Parker paying Ashley's rent for the last six months, and the neighbor mentioned seeing her with other men, possibly even another man who frequents the apartment," Lori summarized.

"Did she give you a description of the other guy?" she asked Shaun.

"No, she didn't get a good look at him. All she knew was that it wasn't John Parker. I showed her a picture of him on my phone," Shaun replied.

The siblings contemplated the implications of this new information. It seemed that Ashley Brenner's life was far more complicated than they had initially assumed. The fact that John Parker had been financially supporting her was certainly a critical piece of the puzzle, but the presence of another man, or even multiple men, in her life raised more questions.

"Whoever this other guy is, we need to find him," Lori said firmly. "He could be a crucial witness or even a suspect."

Shaun nodded in agreement. "I'll start looking into the other people Ashley was connected to. Maybe someone in her circle knows something."

As the investigation continued, Lori and Shaun found themselves drawn deeper into the web of deceit and intrigue surrounding Ashley's life. Each new piece of evidence and every witness interview led them closer to the truth, but also revealed just how many secrets had been hidden in the shadows of Nashville's music scene. And as the trial date drew nearer, the pressure to untangle the mystery and clear John Parker's name only grew more intense.

NINE

Shaun decided to go back to the Blue Bird, hoping to find someone who might know more about Ashley and John's relationship. "The clock definitely isn't on our side. We need to find out what was going on between them," he told Lori before leaving. After asking around, Shaun discovered there was a waitress named Daisy who had worked late nights at the Blue Bird but had since quit. Rumor had it she now worked at Kid Rock's restaurant down on Broadway.

Shaun arrived at Kid Rock's Honky Tonk and Steakhouse, an impressive five-story building with a façade covered in neon lights and flashy signage. The interior was a mix of classic honky-tonk style and contemporary decor, with walls adorned with musical memorabilia and mounted guitars. Each floor offered something unique, from the main stage on the first floor to the private event space on the fourth.

Shaun found Daisy working as a bartender on the fifth floor, which featured a rooftop bar with a stunning view of downtown Nashville. The bustling cityscape stretched out before him, bathed in the warm glow of the setting sun. The rooftop bar was a lively spot, with patrons enjoying drinks and conversation against the backdrop of live country music.

Shaun took a seat at the bar and ordered a glass of water. "You need to order something besides that, or they might throw you out," Daisy warned, her voice tinged with a Southern accent. Shaun hesitated, remembering his parole terms – he wasn't supposed to consume alcohol. It had been three years since his last beer or hit off a vape pen with THC oil. "Coors Light," he finally said, relenting.

Daisy returned with an ice-cold bottle of Coors Light and set it down on a napkin. "Need anything else?" she asked. Shaun took a swig from the bottle and examined the label for a second before asking, "You Daisy?"

"I am, why?" she said, her eyes narrowing with curiosity.

"We need to talk," Shaun replied, his tone serious.

Daisy seemed hesitant, but she eventually agreed to chat with Shaun during her break. As they sat down in a quiet corner of the rooftop bar, Shaun explained his connection to John Parker and his search for information on Ashley Brenner. At first, Daisy seemed guarded, but as Shaun shared more details about the case, she became increasingly forthcoming.

TEN

As Shaun and Daisy continued their conversation, the sun dipped below the horizon, casting a warm glow over the city. The sounds of laughter, clinking glasses, and the strumming of guitars from live bands filled the air, creating a vibrant atmosphere on the rooftop bar at Kid Rock's Honky Tonk and Steakhouse. The energy of downtown Nashville was palpable, the city alive with music and the promise of dreams coming true.

"So, Ashley must've made an impression on someone in the audience at the Blue Bird," said Shaun, leaning in closer to hear Daisy over the noise.

"Everyone goes there to try and get discovered. She wasn't any different," Daisy replied in her Southern accent.

"See her with anyone else in there besides Parker?" asked Shaun.

"No, but I heard her friends talking one night in there about her."

"What'd they say?" asked Shaun, his curiosity piqued.

"They were going on about how she was playing a dangerous game with experienced men. The powerful kind, ones that can hurt you real bad."

"Emotionally or physically?" asked Shaun.

"I don't know, I guess maybe both. I heard they found her dead in that apartment of hers. It was really fancy from what I was told."

"Who are her friends?" asked Shaun.

"I don't know their names. But I seen her hang out with them and talk sometimes at the Blue Bird."

"Have you seen them since?"

"Couple of times, they even came in here the other night."

"So, you'd recognize them if you saw them?"

"Yeah, sure," said Daisy.

Shaun gave Daisy his cell number and told her to call him if they showed up again. As he left the rooftop bar, the dazzling lights of

Nashville twinkling beneath him, Shaun couldn't shake the feeling that he was on the verge of uncovering a dangerous secret. The powerful men Daisy mentioned could hold the key to solving Ashley's murder, and he was determined to find out the truth, whatever the cost.

As Shaun updated Lori on his conversation with Daisy, they knew they had to tread carefully in their investigation. There was a hidden world lurking beneath the surface of the music scene, one where ambition and desire could lead to fatal consequences. With each new piece of the puzzle, the siblings were drawn deeper into the darkness, determined to bring justice to Ashley Brenner and clear John Parker's name.

ELEVEN

Lori was up early and at the office, having stopped by the Frothy Monkey to pick up her favorite Signature latte. The rich aroma of espresso, steamed milk, and caramelized brown sugar filled the air, hinting at the delicious concoction of the Hummingbird latte she had ordered. She had also grabbed a plain black coffee for Shaun, who typically would show up a few minutes after she did.

Lori had her motion to dismiss Parker's charges denied. It had taken her hours to draft it after researching relevant case law, procedures, and then drafting and revising the motion. Shaun knocked on her halfway opened office door and could smell the coffee.

"Thanks for the coffee. I got home late last night and just crashed. I might have a lead on getting more information into Ashley's life. Bartender over at Kid Rock's on Broadway has my number."

"What were you doing there?" asked Lori.

"Daisy who works there used to be over at the Blue Bird. We sat and talked."

"What'd she say?" asked Lori.

"That she only saw Ashley and Parker together, never with any other men, and that her friends were saying she was playing some game. That they were concerned for her," said Shaun.

Lori looked back at her laptop. "Looks like we're going to trial."

"You knew that all along, though, right? That motion wasn't going to stick."

"I owed it to the client to at least try. I still don't know why he picked me."

"Don't start that, you know why," said Shaun.

Lori took a sip of her latte. "That Kemper case sort of made the phone ring a little."

"Didn't hurt, but I thought you would've moved us out of this place," said Shaun.

"We just might if the landlord doesn't start living up to his end of our lease."

"How long has that coffee been there?" asked Shaun, pointing to Lori's desk.

"Only a few minutes," said Lori. "I tried checking Ashley's social media accounts, but they've been scrubbed clean," said Shaun.

"We could use a break," said Lori as she went back to typing on her laptop.

"Drafting another motion?" asked Shaun.

"Good guess, probably the first of many. We're in for a fight. I heard some scuttlebutt in the courtroom hallway about the prosecutor not liking Parker very much."

"That's all we need," said Shaun.

As they braced themselves for the upcoming trial, Lori and Shaun knew they had their work cut out for them. They would need to dig deep into Ashley's life, uncover the secrets she had left behind, and find a way to prove John Parker's innocence. And with the prosecutor harboring a personal vendetta against Parker, the battle would be even more intense.

TWELVE

Lori sat at her desk, the afternoon sunlight streaming through the dirty window, casting a golden glow over the room. Parker's case file lay open next to her, its pages filled with notes, witness statements, and evidence. She couldn't help but notice the specific date mentioned in the arrest warrant: the same date Ashley Brenner had been last seen with John Parker.

That date was the linchpin of the prosecution's case, and Lori knew that her client's alibi and defense had to be airtight. The odds were stacked against them, and the tiniest crack in their story could lead to a guilty verdict. She took a deep breath and began reviewing the details of the night in question.

According to the file, John Parker had been seen with Ashley Brenner at the Blue Bird Cafe earlier that evening. Witnesses reported that they appeared to be having a good time, enjoying each other's company, and sharing drinks. However, Parker claimed that after they left the Blue Bird, they had gone their separate ways. Ashley, he said, had left with another man, while he went home alone.

Lori knew she needed to find evidence to support Parker's story. She needed to find witnesses who could corroborate his version of events, or perhaps even security footage from nearby businesses that might show Ashley leaving with another man. But with each passing day, memories grew fuzzier, and the chances of uncovering such evidence became slimmer.

As Lori dug deeper into the case, she realized that the prosecution's focus on the date of Ashley's murder wasn't a coincidence. It was a deliberate attempt to make it nearly impossible for Parker to provide a solid alibi. The more she studied the case, the more it seemed like a meticulously constructed trap.

With a growing sense of unease, Lori wondered if there was more to the story than met the eye. Was it possible that someone had deliberately framed John Parker for Ashley's murder? And if so, who stood to gain from his conviction?

As the shadows lengthened and the sun dipped below the horizon, Lori continued to pore over the case file, determined to find the answers that could save her client's life. But with each passing minute, the weight of a trial bore down on her, a constant reminder of the high stakes and the lives hanging in the balance.

THIRTEEN

Lori's motion for discovery was finally being heard after several long weeks. The courtroom was a grand, intimidating space with towering ceilings, dark wooden paneling, and rows of stiff, wooden benches. A massive American flag hung behind the judge's bench, its colors bold against the stark, off-white walls. The room hummed with a sense of importance, the air thick with tension.

Alex Thompson, the District Attorney General for Davidson County, stood opposite Lori, prepared to argue against her motion. Thompson was a tall man with a thick head of salt-and-pepper hair, a sharply chiseled jawline, and piercing blue eyes that seemed to bore into the soul of anyone he faced in court. He carried himself with a hint of arrogance, emanating an air of superiority that could be both intimidating and infuriating.

Lori knew that she was in for an uphill battle. As a first-year attorney, she was inexperienced in the nuances of Tennessee's criminal procedures, and the process of obtaining discovery had proven to be a surprisingly difficult and complex ordeal. But she refused to let this deter her. Her tenacity and determination were her greatest weapons, and she would fight tooth and nail for her client.

The prosecution had responded to Lori's motion, objecting to her request and seeking clarification on the scope of the discovery. In accordance with the court's rules and the judge's order, the hearing was scheduled to address the motion. Lori and Thompson would each have the opportunity to present their arguments and respond to questions from the judge.

As the hearing began, Lori presented a compelling case for the defense's need to access the requested materials, emphasizing the importance of a fair and thorough examination of the evidence. Thompson, however, countered with a strong argument, asserting that the scope of Lori's request was overly broad and invasive, potentially jeopardizing the integrity of the investigation.

The judge listened intently to both sides, weighing the merits of their arguments, and asking pointed questions to clarify their positions. After a lengthy and heated exchange, the judge finally issued an oral ruling. Lori's motion was granted in part, with certain modifications to the scope of the discovery to address the prosecution's concerns.

As Lori left the courtroom, she felt a mixture of relief and frustration. While the ruling was a partial victory, the modifications to the scope of the discovery meant that she would have to proceed with caution, working within the confines of the court's order. Nevertheless, she was one step closer to unearthing the truth and securing justice for her client.

The prosecution was now required to comply with the ruling and provide the requested materials to the defense within the specified time frame. Failure to do so could result in sanctions or other consequences. Lori knew that this was just the beginning of a long and arduous legal battle, but she was more determined than ever to see it through to the end.

FOURTEEN

Lori sat in her office, the room lit only by the dim glow of her laptop screen. Outside, a terrible thunderstorm raged, torrents of rain lashing against the window, and the wind howling like a wild beast. The power had gone out for several blocks, including her building, leaving her and Shaun in near-darkness.

On her laptop, Lori watched surveillance footage from Ashley Brenner's apartment. The video was grainy and of poor quality, but it was one of the pieces of evidence provided by the prosecutor's office as part of her motion for discovery. She squinted at the screen, trying to make out the details of the scene.

Shaun leaned in, peering over her shoulder as they both watched a man enter Ashley's building around the time of her murder. The figure was tall, his features obscured by shadows and the low resolution of the footage.

"That doesn't do us a whole lot of good," Shaun muttered, frustration evident in his voice. "Maybe I should check with any other businesses nearby to see if they have any footage."

Lori nodded, her eyes still fixed on the screen. "I'd have to subpoena them for it most likely. But it's worth a shot."

Shaun sighed, glancing out the window at the storm raging outside. "I'll canvass the area when the storm lets up."

"Hopefully the power comes back on soon," Lori added, her voice barely audible above the din of the storm. She replayed the footage again, searching for any clues or details they might have missed. The man in the video remained elusive, a ghostly figure haunting the edges of their investigation.

As the storm continued to batter the city, Lori and Shaun huddled in the dim glow of the laptop, determined to unravel the mystery of Ashley Brenner's murder. The inclement weather seemed to echo the turbulence and darkness that had enveloped their case, and they knew that the path to the truth would be fraught with challenges and uncertainty.

FIFTEEN

Shaun stepped outside, the torrential downpour soaking him within seconds. The skies were a menacing shade of gray, and the heavy rain blurred his vision as he made his way through the deluge. The air was thick with the scent of rain-soaked pavement, and the sound of the downpour drummed in his ears, punctuated by the occasional rumble of thunder.

Undeterred by the relentless rain, Shaun canvassed the neighboring businesses of Ashley Brenner's apartment building, searching for any additional surveillance footage that could shed light on her murder. The power was still out for most of the area, except for a small corner convenience store that was operating on a generator. The store was a beacon of light in the midst of the storm, its neon sign flickering intermittently, casting an eerie glow on the soaked streets.

Inside the store, the clerk was initially reluctant to let Shaun see the footage. However, after some persuasion, he finally agreed to let Shaun view the recording from the night of Ashley's murder. As the video played, Shaun's heart raced with anticipation, hoping for a breakthrough in the case.

There, on the screen, was the same figure from the apartment's footage, but this time captured from a different angle. The mysterious man had parked his car, a newer BMW, on the street. Only part of the license plate was visible, but it was enough for Shaun to jot down the partial plate number.

Excited by this new lead, Shaun thanked the clerk and rushed back out into the storm, immediately dialing Lori's number. "I think I might have something," he shouted over the din of the rain.

What Shaun didn't see, however, was the very same BMW parked about a block away, out of his sightline. Inside the car, its occupant watched Shaun intently, his eyes narrowing as he observed Shaun's every move. It was clear that this mysterious individual was keenly interested in Shaun's actions, and as the rain continued to pour down, the web of intrigue surrounding Ashley Brenner's murder only grew more tangled and complex.

SIXTEEN

The storm had finally passed, and power was restored to Lori's office later that evening. Shaun excitedly burst through the door, armed with the partial plate information and the make and model of the car outside Ashley Brenner's apartment, as captured by the corner store's surveillance footage.

With this new lead, Lori knew she had to act quickly. Despite the late hour, she stayed in her office, meticulously drafting a subpoena for the Department of Motor Vehicles (DMV). She was well aware that attempting to obtain license plate information with only a partial plate number could be a challenging process, but she was determined to uncover the truth.

Lori carefully crafted the subpoena duces tecum, ensuring it provided a reasonable basis for the request and a clear description of the information sought. She knew that with an incomplete plate number, there might be multiple potential matches, or even an inability to identify the correct vehicle. But she pressed on, focused on the possibility of a breakthrough in the case.

As she researched further, Lori recognized the potential legal obstacles she might face, such as the DMV raising concerns about the scope of the request, privacy issues, or the burden of searching for records based on partial information. She understood that the court may need to review her subpoena and determine whether it was appropriate to enforce her request.

Lori also paid close attention to federal and state privacy laws, such as the Driver's Privacy Protection Act (DPPA), which regulated the disclosure of personal information held by the DMV. She knew that in some situations, a court order may be required to access certain DMV records due to privacy concerns. As a defense attorney, she understood the importance of carefully evaluating the legal requirements and restrictions before attempting to subpoena DMV records.

The hours ticked by, and the first light of dawn began to creep through the office window. Exhausted but determined, Lori finally completed the subpoena, ready to face whatever challenges lay ahead in her pursuit of justice for her client. As she sent off the subpoena to the appropriate authorities, she couldn't help but feel a spark of hope that this new lead might finally shed light on the truth behind Ashley Brenner's murder.

SEVENTEEN

Shaun's tiny one-bedroom apartment was a testament to his simple lifestyle. The walls, once white, now bore a yellow tinge from years of neglect. Sparse thrift store furniture, like the mismatched sofa and the worn wooden coffee table, filled the small living area. The threadbare curtains did little to block out the streetlights that cast eerie shadows across the room.

Above him, Shaun's noisy neighbors stomped around, their movements so heavy it felt like they were going to fall through the ceiling at any moment. Muffled arguments and the occasional crashing sound filtered through the thin walls, making it nearly impossible for Shaun to find peace and quiet.

As he lay on his squeaky mattress, trying to block out the cacophony around him, sleep eluded him. His mind raced with thoughts of the case, the mysterious car, and the potential lead at the DMV. Just as he felt himself drifting off to sleep, his body was jolted awake by a sudden hypnic jerk. The involuntary muscle contraction left him wide-eyed and frustrated, his heart pounding in his chest.

It was in this restless state that Shaun's cell phone suddenly vibrated off his nightstand. Startled, he fumbled to grab it, but his fingers slipped in his haste. As it fell to the floor, Shaun managed to flip the screen over and squint at the caller ID. It was Daisy, the bartender from Kid Rock's Honky Tonk.

Quickly answering the call, Shaun could hear the loud music and chatter of the bar in the background. Daisy's voice cut through the noise, telling him that one of Ashley Brenner's friends was there. Shaun's heart raced at the news, but his excitement was tempered by the urgency in Daisy's voice. The young woman was starting to argue with her boyfriend, and it was unclear how long she'd stay now that the fighting had begun.

Wasting no time, Shaun threw on his clothes, grabbed his keys, and bolted out of his apartment. He knew this could be a crucial opportunity to learn more about Ashley's life, and he couldn't afford to miss it. As he raced through the dark streets towards the bar, the weight of the case and the potential for new information pushed him forward, leaving the chaos of his tiny apartment far behind.

EIGHTEEN

Shaun's heart pounded in his chest as he started his car and pulled out of his apartment lot, heading towards downtown Nashville. The adrenaline from the late-night call coursed through his veins, fueling his urgency to reach Kid Rock's Honky Tonk as quickly as possible. His foot pressed down on the gas pedal, pushing the car to speeds that went beyond the legal limit.

The city streets were slick from the recent storm, and the headlights of his car cut through the darkness, reflecting off the wet asphalt. As he sped through the night, Shaun couldn't help but marvel at the sight of Nashville after a rainstorm. The city seemed to come alive in a new way, with the neon lights from bars and restaurants reflecting off the waterlogged streets, creating a kaleidoscope of colors that danced across the pavement.

As he approached an intersection, Shaun noticed a Sheriff's patrol car cruising in the opposite direction. Their eyes met for a brief moment, and he knew he'd been caught. His heart sank as he watched the patrol car's brake lights come on, and he braced himself for the inevitable flashing of red and blue lights.

In his rearview mirror, Shaun saw the patrol car turn into a driveway just beyond the intersection, but it didn't emerge to pursue him. He held his breath, waiting for the officer to reappear, but nothing happened. Relief washed over him as he realized he had narrowly avoided a costly error.

NINETEEN

Shaun raced through the streets of Nashville, his heart still pounding from his near-encounter with the Sheriff's patrol car. As he neared Kid Rock's Honky Tonk, he searched for a parking spot, but found that the area was teeming with nightlife revelers. With time running out, Shaun reluctantly chose to park illegally in a tow-away zone, knowing full well the risk he was taking.

Entering Kid Rock's, Shaun was immediately assaulted by the cacophony of sound – live music blaring from the stage, the hum of conversations filling the air, and the clinking of glasses as patrons enjoyed their drinks. The dim lighting, combined with the multitude of neon signs, gave the place a gritty, electric ambiance.

Shaun made his way to the fifth floor, where he spotted Daisy behind the bar. Her eyes widened in recognition as she quickly pointed him towards a couple engaged in a heated argument. The woman, presumably Ashley's friend, appeared to be in her early twenties, with long, wavy brown hair and a petite frame. The man she was arguing with, also in his twenties, was tall and muscular, with a dangerous glint in his eyes.

Realizing the situation could escalate quickly, Shaun attempted to intervene casually, stepping between the arguing couple and offering to buy them both a drink in hopes of diffusing the tension. The man, however, was not interested in peace. He sneered at Shaun, sizing him up as a potential threat.

"What's it to you, man?" the man spat, his anger fueled by alcohol and jealousy. "You think you can just swoop in and save her?"

Shaun, fully aware of his parole status, tried to keep his cool. "Look, man, I'm not trying to cause any trouble. I just thought we could all enjoy a drink and calm down."

The man's face reddened, his fists clenching as he sized up Shaun once more. "You think you're so tough, huh?" he slurred, lunging forward with a wild swing.

Shaun, with his quick reflexes, sidestepped the punch, causing the man to lose his balance and crash into tables and stools, knocking them over in a cacophony of noise. The entire bar went silent, eyes fixed on the scene.

Seizing the opportunity, Shaun grabbed the woman's hand and led her outside, away from the chaos. As they stepped out into the cool night air, Shaun glanced at the spot where he had parked his car only to find it missing. He cursed under his breath, realizing that it had been towed away in the short time he had been inside the bar.

As they stood on the sidewalk, the woman turned to Shaun, tears streaming down her cheeks. "Thank you for getting me out of there. I don't know what I would've done without you."

TWENTY

Shaun and the woman walked together through the damp streets of Nashville, the city's neon lights casting a kaleidoscope of colors onto the wet pavement. They eventually found themselves outside a small, cozy diner that was still open despite the late hour.

As they entered the diner, they were greeted by the comforting scent of coffee and the low hum of a jukebox playing classic country tunes. They chose a booth near the back, away from the few other patrons who were scattered throughout the establishment.

Once they were settled, the woman introduced herself as Emily. Shaun wasted no time in asking her about the man she had been arguing with earlier, but Emily dismissed him as an overbearing ex-boyfriend who refused to let go.

Shaun then broached the subject of Ashley Brenner and the mysterious man Emily had mentioned in her conversation with Daisy. Emily hesitated for a moment before revealing that the man was a high-powered music executive named Tom Baxter. He had been romantically involved with Ashley and had a reputation for being controlling and possessive.

As they sipped their coffee, Emily explained that Tom and Ashley had met at a music industry event, and their relationship had quickly escalated. However, as time went on, Ashley confided in Emily that she was beginning to feel trapped and wanted to break free from Tom's controlling grip.

Shaun listened intently, sensing that there was more to this story. He asked Emily if she had any idea whether Tom could have been involved in Ashley's murder. Emily hesitated, clearly uncomfortable with the question, but eventually admitted that she couldn't be sure.

"I never really trusted Tom," Emily said, her voice wavering. "He could be so charming and persuasive, but there was always something off about him. Ashley told me once that he had a temper, and she was scared of what he might do if she left him."

Shaun leaned in closer, his eyes focused on Emily as he tried to gauge the truth in her words. "Do you think Tom could have killed Ashley out of jealousy or because he felt threatened by her decision to leave him?"

Emily looked down at her coffee, her hands trembling slightly. "I don't want to believe it, but the more I think about it, the more it seems possible. Tom had the power and connections to make things difficult for Ashley, and she was terrified of him."

Shaun thanked Emily for sharing her story and assured her that he would do everything in his power to bring Ashley's killer to justice. As they left the diner, the first light of dawn was beginning to break through the clouds, casting a soft glow on the city streets.

Determined to follow up on this new lead, Shaun and Emily exchanged contact information, agreeing to stay in touch as the investigation unfolded.

TWENTY-ONE

Shaun stood on the sidewalk, the morning light casting long shadows on the wet pavement. His car was impounded, and he knew he needed to update Lori on the latest developments in the case. Pulling out his phone, he dialed her number, hoping she wasn't too upset by the early hour.

Lori answered groggily, but her tone shifted to one of concern as Shaun recounted his encounter with Emily and the information she had provided about Tom Baxter. Sensing the importance of the new lead, Lori offered to pick Shaun up and drive him home so they could discuss their next steps.

When Lori arrived, Shaun climbed into her car, grateful for her willingness to help him despite the hour. As they drove through the quiet streets of Nashville, Shaun filled Lori in on the details of his conversation with Emily. Lori listened intently, her eyes narrowing as Shaun mentioned Tom Baxter's controlling nature and Ashley's fear of him.

As they pulled up to Shaun's apartment, Lori turned to him, her expression serious. "This new information changes everything. We have a solid lead and a potential motive. We need to tread carefully, but I think we're on the right track."

TWENTY-TWO

Lori arrived back at the office as the sun was just beginning to rise, casting a warm, golden light through the windows. She decided to let Shaun sleep a few more hours, knowing they would need all the energy they could muster to tackle the case with this new information. The impound lots wouldn't be open until 9:00 AM anyway, so there was no need to rush.

Seated at her desk, Lori took a deep breath and began to sift through the prosecution's evidence and witness interviews once again, this time with a keen eye for any mention of Emily or Tom Baxter. She couldn't shake the feeling that there was something off about the way the investigation had unfolded – it seemed almost as though the focus had been deliberately placed on Parker to the exclusion of all other possibilities.

As she read through the documents, Lori's suspicions only grew. The interviews with Emily were cursory at best, with no mention of her concerns about Tom or his possible involvement in Ashley's murder. It was as if the prosecution had tunnel vision, zeroing in on Parker and disregarding any other potential suspects.

The more Lori looked into it, the more she began to wonder if the investigation had been orchestrated to fit a predetermined narrative. Was it possible that someone with influence or power had manipulated the case to ensure that

Parker was the prime suspect and divert attention away from Tom Baxter? Could Tom's connections in the music industry have played a role in swaying the investigation?

Frustrated and concerned, Lori pulled up her contacts and made a few calls, trying to gather any additional information on Tom Baxter. Most of her sources were tight-lipped, but she managed to uncover a pattern of aggressive behavior and a history of using his influence to get his way. It wasn't concrete evidence, but it was enough to give Lori pause.

As the clock ticked closer to 9:00 AM, Lori made a decision. She would dig deeper into Tom Baxter and his possible connection to Ashley's murder. If there was even a chance that he was involved, it was worth pursuing every lead, even if it meant going up against powerful and influential adversaries.

With renewed determination, Lori gathered her things and prepared to pick up Shaun. They had a long day ahead of them, but she was more committed than ever to uncovering the truth and ensuring that justice was served for Ashley Brenner.

TWENTY-THREE

Lori had just finished gathering her things and was about to leave her office to pick up Shaun when she noticed Parker standing in the doorway. He looked tired but determined, and he offered to take her to breakfast. Surprised but grateful for the opportunity to discuss the case with him further, Lori agreed.

They decided on the Pancake Pantry, a well-known Nashville institution famous for its mouth-watering breakfast dishes. As they walked towards the restaurant, the imposing AT&T building came into view. Its distinctive design, often referred to as the "Batman Building" due to its resemblance to the superhero's mask, towered above the surrounding architecture, casting a long shadow across the sidewalk.

Parker held the door open for Lori, and they stepped inside the Pancake Pantry. The interior was warm and inviting, with wooden tables and chairs, and walls adorned with vintage photographs and memorabilia. The aroma of freshly cooked pancakes and bacon filled the air, making Lori's stomach rumble in anticipation.

They settled into a booth near the window, and Parker handed Lori a menu. Scanning the extensive list of options, she decided on the Georgia Peach Pancakes, while Parker opted for the Country Ham and Eggs. As they waited for their food, Lori couldn't help but notice the mix of tourists and locals filling the restaurant, all enjoying their hearty breakfasts.

Parker broke the silence by telling Lori that there were more details he needed to share with her. She replied that his timing was impeccable and cautiously brought up the subject of Tom Baxter. At the mention of his name, Lori noticed a barely perceptible change in Parker's expression, suggesting a hint of jealousy. She asked Parker if he knew that Ashley had been involved with Baxter.

Parker hesitated for a moment before admitting that he had been aware of their relationship, but he didn't know the extent of it. He shared that Ashley had been secretive about her involvement with Baxter, and he had always felt uneasy about the music executive.

Their conversation was briefly interrupted as the server arrived with their food and drinks. Lori couldn't help but admire the sight of her Georgia Peach Pancakes, topped with powdered sugar and fresh peach compote, while Parker's Country Ham and Eggs were accompanied by a generous portion of hash browns and a warm biscuit.

As they continued their discussion between bites, Parker revealed that he had overheard Ashley arguing with Baxter on the phone a few days before her death. He couldn't make out the details, but he could sense the tension and fear in her voice. Parker regretted not pressing Ashley further about her relationship with Baxter or doing more to protect her.

Lori listened intently, processing the information and considering its implications for the case. She reassured Parker that they would follow every lead and do everything in their power to uncover the truth.

TWENTY-FOUR

After an enlightening breakfast at the Pancake Pantry, Lori picked up Shaun from his apartment and drove him to the impound lot to retrieve his car. They arrived at the address listed on the ticket and found themselves at a large, fenced-in lot filled with vehicles of all shapes and sizes. A tall chain-link fence topped with barbed wire surrounded the area, and a small, unassuming office building stood at the entrance. Shaun took a deep breath as they approached the office, steeling himself for the inevitable haggling that was to come. The door creaked loudly as they entered, revealing a cramped space with a worn linoleum floor and flickering fluorescent lights overhead. The walls were adorned with faded posters detailing various towing regulations and policies, and a thick glass partition separated the waiting area from the employee workstations. A woman in her late forties, with graying hair tied back in a tight bun, sat behind the glass. She eyed them suspiciously, chewing gum loudly as she awaited their inquiry. Shaun presented the ticket he had received when his car was towed and asked about the procedure for retrieving his vehicle. The woman, her name tag identifying her as "Janice," tapped a few keys on her computer and informed Shaun of the exorbitant fees he would need to

pay to release his car from impound. Shaun's eyes widened at the numbers she quoted – fees for towing, storage, and administrative costs, which had all accumulated at an alarming rate. He tried to negotiate, arguing that the fees were outrageous and that his car had only been in the lot for a few hours.

Janice remained unyielding, her expression stone-cold as she continued to chew her gum. She informed Shaun that the fees were non-negotiable, and if he couldn't pay, his car would remain in the lot, accruing even more charges each day. Shaun glanced at Lori, who gave him a sympathetic look but knew there was little they could do in this situation.

Feeling defeated, Shaun reluctantly handed over his credit card, watching as Janice swiped it and printed out the receipt. He signed the necessary paperwork, each stroke of the pen feeling like a concession to the towing company's tactics. With the transaction completed, Janice directed them to the area where Shaun's car was located within the lot.

As they walked through the impound lot, Shaun couldn't help but notice the variety of vehicles that had been towed and left there – from expensive sports cars to rusted-out junkers. The gravel crunched under their feet, and the air was filled with the scent of oil and exhaust. The lot was dotted with weeds, and in some areas, car parts were haphazardly stacked in piles, a testament to the chaos of the towing business.

Finally, they found Shaun's car sandwiched between two other vehicles, looking a bit worse for wear but still intact. Shaun sighed with relief as he unlocked the door and slid behind the wheel.

TWENTY-FIVE

As Lori sat in her office, her mind wandered back to the beginning of her involvement in Parker's case. She recalled the day he was arrested and the subsequent legal process that led them to this point. It all started with Parker's arrest and the mittimus issued by the court, directing law enforcement officers to detain him. Following his arrest, Parker was taken into custody and booked at the local jail. At Parker's initial appearance, the judge informed him of the charges against him, his rights, and set the conditions for his release, including bond. Lori remembered how distraught Parker had been during this appearance, his fear and confusion palpable. The case had proceeded to a preliminary hearing, during which the judge determined there was probable cause to believe that Parker had committed the crime. The grand jury subsequently indicted Parker, formally charging him with murder. During Parker's arraignment, he entered a not guilty plea, and the court set a trial date. From that moment, Lori and Shaun had been diligently working on his defense, poring over every piece of evidence and witness statement. During the discovery phase, Lori had grown increasingly concerned about the prosecution's case. It seemed to her that they were laser-focused on Parker, to the exclusion of other potential suspects, like Tom Baxter. In fact, she hadn't seen any indication that Baxter had even been interviewed by the police. This nagging suspicion led Lori to make a call to the prosecutor's office. She politely inquired if they had perhaps forgotten to send over some documents related to Baxter's involvement in the case, hoping to gauge their reaction. The prosecutor's office seemed caught off-guard by her inquiry and hesitated before claiming that they had provided all the relevant documents. However, Lori could sense their uncertainty and was not convinced.

As the trial loomed closer, Lori and Shaun continued to scrutinize the prosecution's case, identifying weaknesses and inconsistencies. They filed several pretrial motions, attempting to suppress evidence and address procedural issues. Meanwhile, plea negotiations were non-existent, as Lori was adamant that Parker would not accept a plea deal. She couldn't shake the feeling that the prosecution was unfairly targeting Parker when another viable suspect was out there.

Lori's determination to uncover the truth and exonerate Parker only grew stronger as they prepared for trial.

TWENTY-SIX

Lori, Shaun, and the prosecution team arrived at the courthouse on the first day of jury selection. They entered the courtroom, where rows of potential jurors were already seated, waiting to be questioned. The diverse group was a cross-section of the community, representing various ages, races, and backgrounds. Lori studied their faces, trying to gauge their openness and ability to be impartial.

The judge called the court to order and provided an overview of the case. He explained the trial process, the role of the jury, and their responsibilities. He emphasized the legal standard of "beyond a reasonable doubt" and the presumption of innocence. The potential jurors listened attentively, some taking notes while others simply observed the proceedings.

The judge then proceeded with the initial questioning, asking the jurors about their backgrounds, experiences, and potential biases. Some jurors were excused for cause, such as personal hardship or clear bias that would prevent them from being impartial. As each juror spoke, Lori and Shaun took notes, discussing their impressions of the jurors and their potential impact on the case.

Once the judge finished the initial questioning, the attorneys were given the opportunity to question the remaining potential jurors. The prosecution went first, asking questions designed to uncover any hidden biases or preconceived notions about the case. Lori and Shaun paid close attention to the jurors' responses and demeanor, looking for any red flags that could negatively impact Parker's defense.

When it was their turn to question the jurors, Lori and Shaun focused on uncovering any potential prejudices against their client, as well as assessing the jurors' ability to remain unbiased in the face of a high-stakes murder trial. They asked about the jurors' experiences with law enforcement, their views on the criminal justice system, and their understanding of the presumption of innocence.

During a short break, Lori and Shaun discussed their impressions of the jurors they had questioned so far.

"What do you think about Juror Number 12?" Lori asked Shaun, looking down at her notes.

Shaun frowned slightly. "She seemed a bit hesitant when we asked about her views on law enforcement. I'm not sure if she'll be sympathetic to our case."

Lori nodded in agreement. "And Juror Number 7 seemed to have a strong opinion about the criminal justice system. He might not be easily swayed by the prosecution's narrative."

As the jury selection process continued, Lori and Shaun continued to evaluate the remaining jurors. They used their peremptory challenges judiciously, striking jurors they believed would be unfavorable to Parker's defense, while the prosecution used their challenges to remove jurors they felt would be sympathetic to the defense.

Finally, after hours of questioning and deliberation, the jury was selected. A panel of twelve jurors and two alternates was chosen, each promising to uphold their duty to remain impartial and weigh the evidence presented during the trial.

With the jury in place, the stage was set for the trial to begin. Lori and Shaun felt cautiously optimistic.

TWENTY-SEVEN

As the pleasant weather continued outside, Lori and Shaun remained focused on the task at hand. They couldn't believe that Tom Baxter's name was on the prosecution's witness list, and it was clear to them that their client was being railroaded. Lori called Parker to her office to get some answers.

"Parker," Lori asked, "What happened in your past that's causing Prosecutor Alex Thompson to come after you so hard?"

Parker hesitated before replying, "Before we each got married, Thompson's wife and I were briefly involved in a romantic relationship. Thompson has always been extremely jealous, and we both belong to the same country club. He can't seem to let go of the past."

Now understanding the potential motivation behind Thompson's aggressive pursuit of Parker, Lori and Shaun realized they needed a new strategy for dealing with Baxter's testimony.

"Shaun," Lori said with determination, "We need to dig deeper into Baxter's background and find a way to use this information about Thompson's jealousy to our advantage during cross-examination."

Shaun nodded in agreement, and they began their research. They combed through Baxter's past, searching for any inconsistencies or questionable connections that might cast doubt on his credibility as a witness.

As the trial approached, Lori's strategy began to take shape. She planned to subtly reveal the connection between Parker and Thompson's wife during her cross-examination of Baxter, without outright accusing the prosecutor of bias. She hoped that by casting doubt on the prosecution's motives, the jury might be more inclined to question the evidence presented against Parker.

During their investigation, Lori and Shaun discovered a few key pieces of information about Baxter's background that they could use to undermine his testimony. They found records of past legal troubles and questionable acquaintances that could potentially implicate Baxter in criminal activities.

As the day of the trial arrived, the pleasant weather outside seemed to reflect Lori's newfound confidence in their strategy. She felt prepared to tackle the challenges that lay ahead and was determined to expose the truth in order to secure justice for Parker.

The trial began, and as Baxter took the stand, Lori focused on executing her carefully crafted cross-examination strategy. As she questioned Baxter about his past, she skillfully wove in reference to Parker's connection with Thompson's wife. By doing so, she hoped to plant seeds of doubt in the jurors' minds about the prosecution's motives.

TWENTY-EIGHT

The courtroom buzzed with anticipation as the trial continued. The diverse jury, a mix of men and women from various walks of life, watched intently as Lori and Baxter faced off. The room was packed with people, from family members to journalists, all eager to witness the unfolding drama. Lori began her cross-examination of Baxter with cordiality, asking about his profession and how long he had lived in the area. She then shifted gears, skillfully dissecting his defenses like a seasoned surgeon. Her questions became more pointed, focusing on Baxter's financial success and the vehicles he owned, including a white BMW. As she held up a document from the Tennessee DMV, Lori revealed that the license plate number of Baxter's white BMW matched the one caught on surveillance footage from a nearby convenience store. The footage showed Baxter's car parked outside Ashley Brenner's apartment building on the night of her brutal murder. The atmosphere in the courtroom grew tense as Lori casually pointed to Baxter's hands, which were scarred and yellowed from small bruises. The jurors exchanged glances, taking note of this potentially incriminating detail. Lori continued her cross-examination, presenting additional footage from inside the apartment building. The video showed both Baxter and Parker at the scene, but Parker had been there much earlier in the

evening. As the evidence mounted against Baxter, his composure began to crack.

Baxter's face reddened with anger, and he glanced accusingly at the prosecution's table. Prosecutor Thompson and his team were visibly shaken, intermittently objecting to Lori's line of questioning, but their objections were swiftly overruled by the judge. The judge found the turn of events intriguing, and the jury was on the edge of their seats, as were the spectators filling the courtroom.

With each revelation, the atmosphere in the courtroom became more charged. The jurors' expressions ranged from shock to disbelief, as they started to question the narrative they had been presented by the prosecution. Lori's relentless cross-examination had skillfully turned the tables, casting doubt on Baxter's credibility and placing him at the center of the investigation.

As Lori wrapped up her questioning, she took one last look at Baxter before returning to the defense table. The courtroom was abuzz with murmurs and speculation, as those present tried to process the explosive new information.

TWENTY-NINE

The final day of John Parker's trial dawned bright and clear. The sun streamed through the windows of the courtroom, casting a warm glow over the proceedings. The room was packed to capacity, as spectators, family members, and journalists jostled for space. John's wife, who had remained silent and distant throughout the ordeal, arrived in support of her husband, finally convinced of his innocence.

As the jurors filed into their seats, the tension in the room was palpable. They carried with them the weight of their decision, one that would forever change the life of the defendant. The judge called the court to order, and the room fell silent in anticipation.

"Members of the jury," the judge addressed them, "have you reached a decision?"

The jury foreperson stood up and replied, "Yes, Your Honor, we have."

The judge nodded and instructed, "Please, read your verdict."

The foreperson cleared their throat and said, "Your Honor, we, the jury, find the defendant, John Parker, not guilty of the charge of murder." A collective gasp filled the courtroom, and John exhaled a sigh of relief that seemed to have been held for an eternity.

Lori and Shaun exchanged triumphant smiles, their hard work and perseverance having paid off. John's wife broke down in tears of joy, and the courtroom erupted into a cacophony of cheers, applause, and whispered conversations.

In the aftermath of the verdict, an arrest warrant was issued for Tom Baxter. The evidence against him had been damning, and it was now his turn to face the consequences of his actions. As he was led away in handcuffs, the enormity of his betrayal became apparent to all.

But the consequences didn't end there. The legal community was rocked by the revelation of Prosecutor Alex Thompson's personal vendetta against John Parker. His blatant disregard for justice in pursuit of a personal agenda led to his disbarment. The disgraced prosecutor left the courtroom with his head hung low, his once-promising career in ruins.

As John Parker embraced his wife and defense team, the sense of vindication was palpable. The long, harrowing journey had finally come to an end, and John was free to rebuild his life, surrounded by those who believed in his innocence.

The sun continued to shine brightly outside the courthouse, reflecting the newfound hope that emerged from the trial's conclusion. In the end, justice had prevailed, and the truth had set John Parker free.

And with that, the dramatic courtroom saga drew to a close, leaving a lasting impression on all who had witnessed it. The story of John Parker's trial would be remembered as a testament to the power of perseverance, the importance of truth, and the triumph of justice over deceit.

MORE COLE STEELE BOOKS
BENEATH DEVIL'S LAKE
THE HARVEST SCAR
CRIMSON ROWS
BRETHREN OF LIBERTY
LINE BREAK
CHAMELEON
DEPARTURE
PROSPECTUS
ADMISSION
ENCOUNTER
PERIL
VESPER
DOSE OF DECEPTION

Don't miss out!

Visit the website below and you can sign up to receive emails whenever Cole Steele publishes a new book. There's no charge and no obligation.

https://books2read.com/r/B-A-AHTI-XPHHC

Also by Cole Steele

Nashville Justice
Dose of Deception
Fatal Verse

Roman Lee
Beneath Devil's Lake
Crimson Rows
Brethren of Liberty
Chameleon
Line Break

Willow Darby
Admission
Encounter
Peril
Departure
Prospectus
Vesper
Reticle

Watch for more at https://www.facebook.com/authorColeSteele.

About the Author

Cole Steele is a versatile and talented author residing in the United States. With a vivid imagination and a knack for storytelling, Cole Steele has successfully created two enthralling book stories and a captivating short story series. Cole Steele is deeply grateful to the writers who first ignited the passion for storytelling and provided the inspiration to embark on this creative journey.

With a commitment to crafting immersive worlds and compelling characters, Cole Steele is delighted to offer readers an escape from the mundane and a chance to embark on exhilarating adventures. The warm reception and love for the characters created by Cole Steele have been both rewarding and motivating.

Cole Steele sincerely hopes that you, too, will join the growing community of readers and find solace, excitement, and inspiration in the characters' journeys. So, prepare to dive into the pages and lose yourself in the enthralling worlds that await you.

Read more at https://realcolesteele.wordpress.com/.

www.ingramcontent.com/pod-product-compliance
Lightning Source LLC
Chambersburg PA
CBHW060504160726
47992CB00003B/1321